OUTSIDE OVER THERE

OUTSIDE

OVER THERE

MAURICE SENDAK

An Ursula Nordstrom Book

Copyright © 1981 by Maurice Sendak
Library of Congress control number: 79-2682
HarperCollins Publishers, New York, NY 10007
Manufactured in China
Calligraphy by Jeanyee Wong
Design by Maurice Sendak and Atha Tehon
19 20 21 SCP 20 19 18 17 16 15 14

For Barbara Brooks

When Papa was away at sea,

and Mama in the arbor,

Ida played her wonder horn
to rock the baby still –
but never watched.

So the goblins came.
They pushed their way in
and pulled baby out,
leaving another all made of ice.

Poor Ida, never knowing, hugged the changeling
and she murmured: "How I love you."

The ice thing only dripped and stared,
and Ida mad knew goblins had been there.

"They stole my sister away!" she cried,
"To be a nasty goblin's bride!"
Now Ida in a hurry

snatched her Mama's yellow rain cloak,
tucked her horn safe in a pocket,
and made a serious mistake.

She climbed backwards out her window

into outside over there.

Foolish Ida never looking,
whirling by the robber caves,
heard at last from off the sea
her Sailor Papa's song:

"If Ida backwards in the rain
would only turn around again
and catch those goblins with a tune
she'd spoil their kidnap honeymoon!"

So Ida tumbled right side round and found herself
smack in the middle of a wedding.

Oh, how those goblins hollered and kicked,
just babies like her sister!

"What a hubbub," said Ida sly,
and she charmed them with a captivating tune.

The goblins, all against their will, danced slowly first,
then faster until they couldn't breathe.

"Terrible Ida," the goblins said,
"we're dancing sick and must to bed."

But Ida played a frenzied jig, a hornpipe
that makes sailors wild beneath the ocean moon.

Those goblins pranced so fierce, so fast,

they quick churned into a dancing stream.

Except for one who lay cozy in an eggshell, crooning and clapping as a baby should. And that was Ida's sister.

Now Ida glad hugged baby tight and she followed the

stream that curled like a path along the broad meadow

and up the ringed-round hill to her Mama

in the arbor with a letter from Papa, saying:

"I'll be home one day,
and my brave, bright little Ida
must watch the baby and her Mama
for her Papa, who loves her always."

Which is just what Ida did.